D1504806

we are NOT buying a camper!

A Frannie Shoemaker
Campground Mystery

by Karen Musser Nortman

Cover Design by Aurora Lightbourne

TABLE OF CONTENTS

PROLOGUE

OCCASIONALLY LATE AT NIGHT, Larry and Frannie Shoemaker and Mickey and Jane Ann Ferraro depart from their usual analyses of national politics and rehash of local gossip around the campfire to reminisce. Their voices low and laughter subdued, they stare into the flames with occasional burst of sparks and recall earlier trips, parties, family events, and how they became camping buddies twenty or so years earlier.

They were related ever since Mickey married Larry's sister. But the Shoemakers were very reluctant to join the Ferraros on their camping weekends.

There're the bugs, they said. And unpredictable weather. And all of the preparation. And, oh yeah, the bugs. Larry and Frannie said it couldn't possibly be worth it.

Yet here they are, after years of camping adventures together — some more exciting than they needed to be — stirring the fire and the memories.

Sometimes Larry blames Mickey for all he has spent on camping and Mickey retorts that those memories are priceless. Other times Larry claims that the Ferraros would have given up camping years ago if the Shoemakers hadn't been there to enhance the events. And Frannie reflects that she wouldn't trade these experiences — even Larry and Mickey's arguments — for anything.

But always the four end up agreeing that it is a marvel that the Shoemakers ever came back after the first two trips.

CHAPTER ONE

"MRS. SHOEMAKER?"

Frannie turned from the filing cabinet. "Yes, Hayden?"

"Um, we're going to be gone on vacation the last week of school and my mom said to ask if I would miss anything."

Frannie smiled sweetly. "Why, no, Hayden, if you aren't going to be here, we won't be doing anything." Sometimes sarcasm was the only way of getting through to eighth graders.

He looked skeptical. "You're kidding, right?"

Frannie sat down at her desk. "Yes, I'm kidding. We'll be reviewing the whole semester for the final test the last day."

"So, I can't really make that up, right—except the test?"

"Sure you can. The last week you are here, we can meet after school every day for review and you can take the test on that Friday."

"But I have the track banquet that week and I need to get my driver's permit after school one day."

"You need it for some job or something?"

"Nooo—but otherwise I can't get it until we get home."

Frannie sighed. "Sometimes I've substituted an alternate assignment, especially if you're going to visit a historical site. Where are you going?"

"Disney World."

"Okay, we'd better stick with the review and the test. I'll give your mom a call this weekend and we'll work out a time for the review." One of the advantages of teaching in a small town was knowing most of the parents.

Hayden grimaced and slouched out of the room.

When she reached the teacher's lounge of the Perfection Falls Middle School, the laughter bubbling out of the door indicated that Mickey Ferraro was holding his usual Friday afternoon court. The small room, used to store supplies in its previous life, was ringed with utilitarian metal-framed chairs, a small refrigerator, and a wooden table holding a typewriter with a dusty plastic cover. Red-faced Kristi Burns, an attractive blonde first year teacher, seemed to be the target of Mickey's relentless teasing, but she also struggled to contain her laughter.

"Mickey, leave the poor girl alone," Frannie said.

Don Whitey, one of the coaches, said, "You should have heard him, Frannie, he said—"

"Aw, she knows I'm kidding and she's a good sport," Mickey interrupted.

"Well, after I call Hayden Brown's mother tonight, I'll call Jane Ann and have her straighten you out."

It didn't faze Mickey. He leaned forward in his chair.

4

"Hey, that reminds me, Jane Ann wanted me to ask you what you guys are doing Memorial Day weekend?"

"Lord, I don't know. That's three weeks away. Why?"

"We're going camping at Honey Lake and we want you guys to go along."

"Camping? Are you kidding? Larry hates camping."

"Jane Ann says he camped all the time with the Scouts when he was growing up. You guys have a tent, don't you?"

Frannie pushed her hair back from her face. "Somewhere. We've never used it except a couple of times when the kids had sleepovers in the back yard. I'll mention it, but don't count on us."

"Think about it. It would be great."

As FRANNIE FOLDED LAUNDRY that evening, Larry walked in from the garage. He unsnapped his holster from his belt, put it and his police revolver in a small cabinet and locked it. His Perfection Falls Police Department shirt was rumpled and stained. He looked at Frannie's face.

"Rough day?"

She straightened up from trying to separate fifteen-year-old Sam's and fourteen-year-old Sally's athletic socks. She couldn't tell the difference, although they always knew if they didn't get the right ones. Giving up, she dumped the pile in an empty basket. Let them work it out.

"The usual end-of-the year craziness. One kid,

Hayden Schultz—you know, Diane and Gary's kid—told me they're going on vacation the whole last week of school. So the week after next, I'm going to have to review him and give him his test before he goes. They couldn't wait a week? And," she laughed and shook her head, "Mickey wanted to know if we want to go camping with them Memorial Day weekend. I told him not likely."

Larry put his hands on his hips and looked at the calendar hanging above the clothes dryer.

"Damn."

"What?" Frannie said.

"Well, a month or so ago, he asked me about it during golf. It's Jane Ann's fortieth birthday that weekend so I told him we'd think about it." He grinned sheepishly at her. "I forgot to mention it to you."

"And I forgot about her birthday coming up. But I thought you always said you hated camping..."

"I don't hate it—but there's a lot of things I would rather do."

"Like golf."

"Like golf," he agreed.

"But what about the kids? I mean Sally can hang out with Mona and Justine, but Sam would kind of be outnumbered." Mona Ferraro was a year older than Sally, and Justine a year younger. The girls had always been close, and Sam the odd man out, literally.

"He could take a friend. Trent would probably love to go. It is a six-person tent, you know." He grinned.

Frannie couldn't believe they were having this

conversation. "We don't have enough sleeping bags for all of us."

"We'd have to borrow a couple. Let's think about it anyway."

AS THEY EXPECTED, Sally was thrilled with the idea; Sam not so much.

"The pool is supposed to open that weekend and Ashley said she's going to have a pool party."

"If it wasn't Aunt Jane Ann's birthday, we probably wouldn't even be thinking about it," Frannie told him. "Summer's barely started—there'll be more parties." It was hard encouraging him to be enthusiastic when she wasn't excited herself.

"I suppose," he said.

Over supper with the Ferraros on Saturday night, Jane Ann practically begged them to go.

"Honey Lake is a great park. It'll be the perfect chance to relax with the end of school and all. You'll be amazed. And they have all kinds of activities planned for the kids because of the holiday."

Frannie didn't expect it to be relaxing, but she couldn't turn Jane Ann down. They had been best friends ever since Frannie and Larry were married.

Jane Ann, a surgical nurse who reminded Frannie of Grace Kelly, had welcomed Frannie into the large, boisterous Shoemaker family. Frannie had been an only child and was a little overwhelmed with the noisy, teasing bunch. Jane Ann became her protector, warding off her siblings when she could see a shell-shocked look come in to Frannie's eyes.

She had come to Frannie's rescue when Sam was born, and Frannie had lugged food and lent support when the Ferraros adopted their two daughters as toddlers. Mickey taught English and Frannie Social Studies to the same group of eighth graders. The two couples had been virtually inseparable. Thus, her capitulation.

On Sunday afternoon, Larry found the box with the tent in the back of the garage, and he and Sam dragged it out into the yard. Frannie took a glass of iced tea out to supervise from a lawn chair.

Larry hung onto the box while Sam pulled the smelly mass of canvas onto the ground.

"Ew, gross! Looks like it's got mildew all over it. Stinks, too."

"It's not too bad," Larry said. "We'll set it up and scrub it down with bleach. A couple of days in the sun, and it'll be fine."

Frannie decided to go back inside.

THEY ASSIGNED SALLY to scare up more sleeping bags. Mickey, an accomplished cook, made up menus and gave Larry a grocery list. Frannie buried herself in end-of-the-year grading, going to the kids' concerts and ball games, and keeping a minimum of order in the house.

She had just finished frosting a cake to take to the Fine Arts Banquet when Sam came in, reached over, and swiped a finger full of frosting from the cake.

"Sam! I have to take that tonight and I don't have time to refrost it!"

He licked his finger and picked up the frosting knife from the counter. With a flourish, he tried to repair the damage. When he was done, the cake looked like it had been hit by a meteor, but he seemed pleased by the result.

"Trent said he can go camping with us. That'll make the truck pretty crowded, so I was thinking I could drive your car, and we could follow you guys."

"You don't have a license. Does Trent have his yet?"

"No, but I have my permit and if we follow you, you'll be able to keep an eye on us."

"You know one of us has to be in the same car when you're driving. Get out of here!" She grinned at him, but after he left, sadly surveyed the cake.

BY THE THURSDAY before Memorial Day, Larry had cleaned out three coolers and Frannie organized her fridge with packages of hot dogs and steaks, containers of fruit, and condiments for the trip.

Friday was the last day of school. By the time Frannie got home, she was exhausted. She dumped her briefcase full of tests in the home office. They could wait until her return from what she mentally labeled That Disastrous Camping Trip. She wondered for the umpteenth time why she had agreed to this. Even the thought of staying home and kicking back in her recliner to grade papers had more appeal.

Larry filled the coolers with ice and sent Sally to collect the refrigerated food. They loaded the coolers into the back of the already-stuffed pickup bed. Sam and Trent arrived and added gym bags sprouting their Walkmans to the mix, shoving and poking each other.

Sally watched them with disgust. "Do I have to ride with them? Can't I ride with Mona and Justine?"

Frannie nodded. "If they have room."

They arrived at the Ferraros. Their SUV sat hooked up to their popup trailer.

Sally bolted from the truck and raced up the driveway. "Aunt Jane Ann! Can I ride with you guys?"

Jane Ann glanced at the Shoemaker vehicle, saw the two boys wrestling in the back seat, and smiled. "You bet. I wouldn't want to ride in there either."

Sally ran back for her bag. By the time she returned, her cousins had made room and beckoned her in, giggling of course. The girls presented a contrasting picture. Sally was a strawberry blonde, compliments of her father, with Frannie's fair skin. She looked more like she could be Jane Ann's daughter. Mona and Justine had dark eyes, deep brown skin, and curly dark hair.

Mickey came out of the house and sauntered down to talk to Larry.

"It's only about an hour. Just follow us."

Finally on the road, Frannie recalled the only time she had been to Honey Lake. The kids were little and they had gone for a family picnic. She remembered bugs.

"Larry," she said, "I forgot to bring any bug spray."

"Relax, Jane Ann will have some."

CHAPTER TWO

IT WAS A LONG HOUR. Frannie kept thinking of other things she should have brought. Finally they entered the park and then the campground. Mickey led them to two campsites he had reserved along the lake.

While Larry and the boys tackled the tent, Frannie surveyed the area. From their sites, the campground spread up a steep hill along gravel access roads that ran parallel to lake shore. The late afternoon sun cast soft shadows across the lake and a light breeze ruffled the grasses along the water. Huge old cotttonwoods, maples, and oaks shaded the area.

Clumps of field daisies filled a ditch running toward the lake. Frannie's mother had always called them "Decoration Day Daisies" and planted them on the grave of her father—a pilot who had been killed in the Korean War.

Jane Ann and Mickey had efficiently opened their popup and completed the setup. Larry and the boys had the tent up, but Larry stood with two short pieces of aluminum in his hands and scratched his head.

Sam unzipped the door and stepped inside just as the whole thing collapsed around him. From under the pile of canvas, he yelled, "I found where those pieces go, Dad!"

It took a few minutes before Trent and Sally could stop laughing long enough to help pull him back out the door. Once Larry was satisfied that the tent would hold for the weekend, Frannie helped unload the rest of the supplies and sleeping bags.

Mickey got supplies together to start a fire. He leaned over the rusty ring and pulled a long white bone out of the ashes. "Well! Apparently someone in the last group of campers must have gotten sassy with the leader. Let this be a lesson to you all!"

Frannie stared. "That isn't—?"

Mickey gave an evil laugh. "Who knows?"

Sam looked over at his uncle. "Cool!"

Frannie shuddered. She thought of the mystery she was currently in the middle of. A family was being stalked through the woods by a killer. Maybe not the best reading material for a camping trip.

Larry rolled his eyes. "Don't believe him, honey. It's an animal bone—maybe a deer."

"How do you know? You're no wildlife expert. Kind of spooky anyway. Why would it be there?"

"Relax. You read too many mysteries."

Mickey laughed. "You better help me cook or you could end up the same."

The plan was for a simple supper. Mickey grilled burgers and Jane Ann added a cast iron pot of cowboy beans to the fire. Frannie grated potatoes for a pile of hash browns into a large cast iron skillet. Mickey instructed her on the amount of oil and temperature of

12

the pan; then growled as she struggled to flip the potatoes and took over on the spatula.

Seated at the picnic table, Frannie began to relax. Nature had cooperated with a fairly bug-free evening and the food hit the spot.

Mickey achieved just the right crispness with the hash browns and left the burgers juicy and slightly rare. Frannie took a big bite of the burger layered with lettuce, tomato, and onion and let the juice run down her chin.

"Mick, you're kind of getting the hang of this cooking thing." Larry spoke around a mouthful of his own burger. Frannie almost choked on hers at his words— Mickey had always been the gourmet in the family.

The five teenagers provided the entertainment. The girls reported on a funny mishap at softball practice and the heart-rending breakup of a friend and 'the only guy she would ever love.'

Trent and Sam countered with a defense of 'the guy' and challenged that track practice was much more difficult than softball. After supper, Jane Ann filled the Dutch oven from a nearby faucet and put it on the fire to heat for dishes.

Frannie looked at Mickey. "I assume there are restrooms? It's going to be a long weekend if there aren't."

He laughed and pointed up the hill at a long, low building. "Up there. Showers, too."

Frannie turned and trudged up the hill, cutting between campsites in order to take the most direct route.

She nodded at others eating supper, sitting around campfires, or playing cards.

She noticed the many original uses of outdoor lights and outrageous lawn ornaments. Decor that would be tacky in a neighborhood seemed fun and fanciful in a campground. A few people gave her disapproving glances, probably explained when Mickey later told her that it was considered bad etiquette to cut through occupied campsites.

At the top of the hill, she walked around the front of the building which faced away from the lake. Larry had just pulled into the small parking lot.

Frannie leaned over, hands on her knees, to catch her breath. "You drove up here?"

"I'm not walking up that hill. But I'll give you a ride back if you want." He winked at her.

"Wimp!" She walked into the women's side of the building.

They returned down the hill to their campsite. Mickey had built the campfire up to a blaze and Sally had pulled out the makings for s'mores. Sam and Trent were already roasting marshmallows.

"Mom! Where's the graham crackers?"

"They should be with the marshmallows and candy bars, in the same box."

Sally set a large box up on the table. "I can't find them."

Frannie joined her and rummaged through the box. No sign of graham crackers. She remembered that the last time she saw them, they were on the kitchen counter. "Well, we'll pick some up tomorrow."

Sam held his stick up and blew out the flaming marshmallow. "Uh, Mom."

"Just put it between two pieces of Hershey," Frannie said.

That tactic was moderately successful, but the kids all ended up with chocolate faces and hands. Jane Ann brought out a plastic tub of soapy water because both Larry and Mickey refused to allow any of them in their vehicles for a ride up the hill to the restrooms. After a basic wash up, they raced each other up the hill to finish the job.

The adults relaxed around the fire and Mickey picked out a few old folk tunes on his guitar, some soulful, some rousing. They sang along on the familiar ones like "This Land is Your Land" and "Blowin' in the Wind." The smoke from the campfire wafted slowly back and forth almost in time to the music.

Jane Ann leaned over to Frannie. "Beautiful, isn't it? I'm so glad you came."

"It is lovely. More relaxing than I expected."

Mickey rubbed his hands together. "Time for ghost stories?"

"Dad!" Mona said. "Tell 'em about the man who murdered his wife."

"Not in a campground, I hope," Frannie said.

"Oh yeah," Justine chimed in. "Tell how you solved it, Dad!"

Frannie looked at Mickey. Obviously, if this was true, they would have heard about it a long time ago. Had to be a joke.

Mickey crouched down by the fire, stirring the embers with a stick. "We were camped over at Barton Falls. The couple next to us argued all day long. Doors slamming, the whole nine yards. We were about to report it to the ranger, but then it got quiet. Not a sound all evening. By the time we went to bed, I was convinced that one of them had done away with the other." He paused and stared into the fire.

"What happened?" Sally demanded.

"The next morning I'm out by the fire early having a cup of coffee. It's just starting to get light. The door of the camper opens and the man steps out and looks around, real sneaky-like. He couldn't see me because of the shadows. He turns around and pulls a roll of carpet out and lugs it over to the dumpster. Then he hurries back to the camper and closes the door."

"So what did you do ?" Trent asked.

"I waited a few minutes, and when he didn't come back out, I got a flashlight and went over to the dumpster."

Frannie sat forward in her chair. "C'mon! Did you look inside the carpet roll?"

"Yes." Mickey looked around at the group, dead serious. An unusual expression for him.

"What was in it, Ferraro?" Larry asked. "Quit dragging this out."

"Nothing."

"Nothing?" This was a chorus from Larry, Frannie, Sam, Sally and Trent. Jane Ann, Justine and Mona giggled and covered their mouths.

Mickey shrugged. "Just a roll of old carpet. I talked to the guy later. Seems the argument was about whether to replace the flooring in their trailer. The wife wanted a new camper. He won and decided to remove the old stuff before she could change her mind."

"So why was he acting so sneaky?" Sally wanted to know.

"I know," Frannie said.

Mickey reverted to classroom mode. "Yes, Mrs. Shoemaker?"

"There's a sign on the dumpster that you can be fined for dumping household items in there."

"Correct!" Mickey said. "You get a star on your forehead."

"I can't believe someone would remodel their camper in a campground," Sam said.

Mickey gave an evil laugh. "You'd be surprised what goes on in a campground."

Larry got up. "If you're done with your tall tales, we'd better get the sleeping bags arranged in the tent. Then I'll make one more trip up the hill for bathroom chores if anyone wants a ride."

Larry had brought one air mattress for him and Frannie, so he laid it in the tent and brought in a small compressor. Once the mattress was inflated, Frannie supervised the arrangement of the sleeping bags.

"How come you guys get an air mattress and we don't?" Sally asked.

"Because we're older and make more money than you do," Larry said. In spite of the tent being fairly good-sized, they shuffled around each other, ducked elbows, and stepped on toes. Frannie tried to ignore the faint bleach smell coming from the canvas.

She had no problem falling asleep.

THE NEXT MORNING, she woke up first and crawled out of the bag. She slipped on a hooded sweatshirt and her moccasins. The sun was up and Mickey had coffee going in a big enamel pot on the fire.

"Hey, I wasn't sure anyone was ever going to join me out here." He pulled a mug from a tote and poured it full of the steaming brew.

Frannie stretched and gratefully accepted the coffee. "Thanks, Mick. I need this badly."

"Did you sleep all right?"

"I think so. I was really beat."

"I hear you. What time should we plan breakfast?"

She looked at him. "I only brought cereal and donuts."

"Maybe not." He pointed toward the Shoemakers' large cooler sitting beside their tent. It was open and tipped over, with the contents strewn around the ground.

"What the—?" Frannie said and walked toward it. "Someone did this in the night?"

"If you include raccoons as *someone*."

"But it was latched." She picked up an empty milk carton and the shredded plastic bag that had held the donuts. Soda cans lay empty, crushed or pierced by sharp little claws.

"They can open anything. I should have had you put it back in your truck or at least pile something heavy on top of it last night. But never fear—I have stuff for bacon, pancakes, and eggs—enough for everyone."

"Now I'm embarrassed. And our steaks for tonight are gone, too." Her frown deepened as she looked in vain around the area for the missing meat.

"Don't be." He leaned forward over the fire to refill his own mug. "I'll put you to work." Then he lowered his voice. "The girls and I decided we're not going to mention Jane Ann's birthday for a while—let her think we forgot."

"That's mean."

Mickey stirred the fire. "Just heightens the suspense."

THE BREAKFAST WAS A HUGE HIT with all of the campers. Frannie marveled at Mickey's organization. With a lack of kitchen counters or a traditional stove, he juggled mixing bowls, serving dishes and cooking utensils on a storage tote turned upside down. He produced a hot breakfast with no leftovers.

"We need to get some meat for supper, since the coons will be enjoying ours," Frannie told Larry.

"If you're going to town, I wouldn't mind riding

along," Jane Ann said. "I forgot to bring dressing for the salad tonight."

Sally, Mona, and Justine decided to hit the beach a short distance from the campground. Trent and Sam announced they were going to hike around the lake. Jane Ann shared bug spray with all.

"We need to get more pop and beer, too, thanks to our masked friends," Larry said.

Mickey stood up and threw up his arms. "We'll all go! Road trip! You driving, Shoemaker?"

"Of course, you mooch." They ribbed each other all the way to the truck.

The nearest town was Bladesburg and the local grocery store was Bob's Bargain Barn. They split up to cover their list. Larry went to peruse the selection at the meat counter while Frannie tracked down the bug spray. With that item secured, she went to find Larry. She grabbed him by the arm.

Larry started. "Careful, I get accosted by women in these stores all the time. It's made me pretty jumpy."

Frannie snorted. "Right. I just thought of something. We've got to do something about a cake for Jane Ann tonight."

He picked up two packages of rib eyes. "We passed a bakery coming in. I could come back — make some excuse — and get a cake."

Frannie shook her head. "It's so warm today and we don't have anywhere to keep it where it won't get ruined. Besides, I saw that place, too, and there was a closed sign in the window."

"I'll find something." He headed toward the bakery department.

She caught up with him as he loaded a pile of packaged cupcakes and Twinkies into a cart.

He handed her the keys. "I'll find some candles and we can stack these up to make a cake. Put your stuff in here and go wait for Mickey and Jane Ann to finish. You can let them in the truck so they don't watch me check out."

Mickey and Jane Ann stood in the checkout line.

Frannie gave Jane Ann the keys. "Larry is agonizing over which kind of steak, so go ahead when you're done. We'll be out in a few minutes."

Mickey started to leave the line. "He probably needs my advice."

"Get back in line," Frannie ordered. "If you go back there, it'll take even longer."

"Yes, ma'am." He saluted.

She shook her head and moved over to peruse a magazine rack.

The Ferarros went out and Larry finally peaked around the corner. "Is the coast clear?"

"Yup. Good thing I brought my canvas shopping bag so she can't tell what we have."

Larry smirked. "I found some of those candles that you can't blow out. You know, they keep relighting."

"You are such a good brother." Frannie started unloading the cart onto the conveyor belt.

They made it back to the campground without Jane

Ann appearing suspicious. Frannie moved the sacks into their tent and returned to the area around the fire. Larry rummaged in the back of his truck for fishing gear, while Mickey got a pole ready.

"Want to walk down to the beach and see how the girls are doing?" Frannie asked Jane Ann.

"Sure. I know they'll be glad to see us — especially if there're any boys there." She grinned and redid her ponytail to remedy stray hair flying around her face.

The path to the beach led through trees and underbrush. Frannie enjoyed the sun playing among the leaves, but kept an eye open for snakes. They reached the beach area and were surprised to find a fairly large crowd. Their daughters were at the far end, sitting on beach towels. Jane Ann's prediction was right. Two teenaged boys sat next to them. The girls laughed as the boys staged a shoving match for their appreciative audience.

Sally said to the others, "I'm getting warm. Let's go in the water." She looked up. "Oh, hi, Mom! This is Greg and Brian. They both play football for Jackson City." She stuck out her tongue at them and then laughed. Jackson City was Perfection Falls' major rival in football.

"Yeah, you just wait 'til next fall," one of the boys said.

The girls got to their feet, brushing off sand, and Mona dashed toward the water. "Last one in's a rotten egg!" In spite of the football rivalry, or because of it, the boys followed.

Frannie and Jane Ann moved back to the edge of the beach, under overarching trees, and found seats on a huge log. The sun sparkled on the water and the musical laughter of the bathers reached them.

Frannie stretched out her legs and leaned back on her arms. "Beautiful."

"Isn't it? Really, you guys should join us more often."

"I know." Frannie sighed. "It is nice, but a lot of work for a little relaxation. Besides, Sam is so busy in the summer with baseball, and — you know."

"Excuses, excuses," Jane Ann said.

"I just can't see Larry going for it on a regular basis."

"Maybe not."

They watched the frolicking on the beach and in the water. Then Jane Ann checked her watch. "I probably should go get the lunch stuff out."

They ambled back to the campsite. Frannie followed Jane Ann's directions to locate sandwich material when a brown Department of Natural Resources truck pulled up. The ranger got out, followed by Sam and Trent.

"These two belong to you?"

"What did they do?" Frannie countered.

"Mom," Sam said. "Why would you say that?"

The ranger put his foot up on the picnic table bench, rested one arm on his knee, and clasped his hands. "They just got a little lost."

"We weren't lost exactly," Trent said. "We weren't sure where we were."

"We got turned around when we crossed the dam,"

Sam said. "Guess what Mom! There's a fishing contest this afternoon and a scavenger hunt."

The ranger smiled at them. "Well, good luck. I'll leave you to your lunch."

"Did you bring fishing gear?" Frannie asked Sam.

"I think Dad did. Hey, Dad!" Sam loped toward the dock, where Larry and Mickey were putting away their gear. Trent followed. By the time they reached the dock, they were trying to push each other in the lake.

Frannie sighed and looked at Jane Ann. "Hopeless."

As the men returned to the campsite, Mickey scoffed at the lunch makings arranged on the picnic table.

"You were assuming we cavemen wouldn't provide a fish lunch for our beloved families?"

Jane Ann raised her eyebrows and looked at him sideways as she continued to set out food. "Were we wrong?"

"Welll—"

"Sam, go fetch the girls from the beach," Frannie said. The boys took off on a run again. "Wish they'd move that fast when I have a real job for them."

CHAPTER THREE
EARLY TUESDAY NIGHT

BEDLAM REIGNED for the next half hour as campers elbowed for room around the picnic table, making sandwiches and snatching packages of lunch meat and jars of peanut butter out of other greedy hands.

"Men first," Sam said, hugging the bread to his chest. "We've been on a wilderness trek while you girls have been laying around getting sand in your brains."

"And we are going to wallop you this afternoon in the scavenger hunt and the fishing contest," Trent added.

Sally grabbed for the bread. "You're smashing it, you dodo."

"Sticks and stones..." Sam began in a sing-song voice.

"And no way you'll beat us this afternoon," Justine said.

The banter continued with no clear winner as sandwiches and chips disappeared at a record rate. Sally got up from the table and threw her paper plate in the fire. "Gotta go take a shower!" Mona and Justine followed.

"A shower...before you go fishing?" Larry said.

"Daa-ad. My hair!" Sally ran a hand through wet tangled curls.

"So? It's fishing, Sal..."

Frannie put down her braunschweiger and horseradish mustard on rye—her favorite—and laid a hand on Larry's arm. "Dear, we've discussed this before." Her tone was mock exasperation. "Don't try to apply logic to anything a teenager says or does."

"Never try to teach a pig to sing," Mickey began, and the rest of the adults joined in shouting, "It wastes your time and annoys the pig!"

Sam shook his head and looked at them in disgust. "That's just stupid. You can't teach a pig to sing."

"Exactly," Jane Ann said.

The girls emerged from tent and popup with towels around their necks and pull-string bags bulging with bottles. Justine swung hers by the cord as she started to narc on her older sister.

"Mona's gotta look good" — the bag described a large arc toward the road and headed back—"for Bry-yun" — she swung the bag again barely missing Sally —"her new boyfriend." The bag rotated back toward the road.

A pop sounded as the seam ripped. A full bottle of "Sweet and Sexy" lavender gel with infused rosemary and cucumbers rocketed out of the bottom of the bag, into the path of an oncoming red GMC Sierra.

The driver was following the five-mile-per-hour campground speed limit, but apparently only glimpsed the purple bomb with his peripheral vision. He slammed on the brakes anyway, stopping on the bottle with his right front tire. A stream of purple goo arced back toward the campsite, hitting Trent square in the back. He had been quietly minding his own business as he fixed himself a third sandwich.

"Hey!" Trent reached back and wiped his shirt, looking at his hand in wonder.

The parents had watched the sequence of events with open mouths. Finally, Mickey snapped his mouth shut and then grinned at his daughter. "Bet you can't do that again."

Justine stood with her hands over her mouth. The cord of the broken bag dangled from her wrist and the rest of her shower items puddled at her feet.

The pickup driver got out of the truck, looking both angry and baffled. He was a tall, balding man with the start of a pot belly. He pushed the cap back on his nearly bald head and scratched his brow. "What was that?"

Everyone started to talk at once, except Justine, who dissolved in tears, and Mona, doubled in laughter.

"Whoa!" The driver's brow cleared and he held up his hands. He looked down at the ground by his truck tire. "Is that shampoo? Is someone throwing a bottle of shampoo?"

Mickey stood up and walked over. He explained the curious order of events and the driver nodded, shook his head, and returned to his truck.

Mickey put his arm around Justine. "Maybe just carry your stuff up to the shower? No swinging?"

She nodded and started to giggle.

Mona said, "Just use mine," and pulled her sister

behind her up the hill.

"Well, Mick," Frannie said, "I admit this camping is pretty fun. What do you have scheduled next?"

Mickey shrugged. "We couldn't duplicate that stunt in a million years."

AN HOUR LATER, the kids gathered at a nearby shelter, where two rangers handed out lists for the scavenger hunt. One ranger didn't look much older than Sam and Sally, and his short hairstyle and bangs didn't add to his age or dignity.

The female ranger was short and in her thirties with blond curly hair. Both were dressed in brown pants and crisp tan shirts, which sported Department of Natural Resources patches on the sleeves.

Though the other adults stayed at the campsite, Frannie had trailed behind the kids and stood at the outer edge of the shelter. She was curious how the hunt was going to work. Justine got herself on a team of four with the romantic Brian, while Mona and Sally teamed up with two older girls.

"Could I have your attention?" The female ranger climbed on a picnic table bench and raised her hands to try and quiet the group. It worked only partially, so she resorted to the whistle worn around her neck.

"Take a look at your lists. Five items have stars by them — see that?"

The kids ducked their heads over the sheets of paper and began nodding.

28

"Those are items that you must not remove—flowers, rocks, etc. If you do, we have to throw you in jail and it will ruin your weekend." She smiled and waited for a few half-hearted laughs.

"Instead, take a photo of the items. We'll use those to judge the winners. Got that? You—in the Batman tee shirt. What are you supposed to do about the starred items on the list?"

A tall thin boy with a halo of flyaway curls jerked his head around, interrupting a conversation with his buddy. "Who, me?"

A short, heavier kid on the other side of him tentatively raised his hand.

The ranger nodded at him. "Can you help your friend out?"

"Um-take pictures of them."

"Right. Everyone got that? Any team that can't get a digital camera?"

One group raised their hands after conferring. "Okay, you guys stop up here before you go out. Any questions?" She looked at her watch. "Everyone meet back here in one hour. That's 2:30, okay?"

The conversation level returned to a dull roar, as the kids headed in various directions. Frannie rolled her eyes at the ranger and returned to her campsite.

Trent and Sam were already there along with two girls. "Okay," Sam was saying. "I have a camera—we need a bag to collect things in. And do either of you have a thermos along?" he asked one of the girls.

29

"I think my mom does."

"And I think we've got a can of beans," the other said.

"Okay, go get them. I'll find a bag, and we've got a flashlight. Meet back by the gate. We'll go to the beach to find a shell and then go from there. Go!"

"Kind of bossy," Frannie said.

Sam shrugged. "Someone's gotta take charge."

Frannie and Larry exchanged amused looks.

"There's an old shopping bag in the truck," Frannie said to Sam.

He and Trent trotted off.

Frannie and Jane Ann carried lawn chairs to the edge of the lake and let the men deal with the marauding groups of kids looking for everything from marshmallows to bug spray. A soft breeze blew off the lake and the happy, challenging voices receded to the background.

Jane Ann sipped her iced tea. "This is what it's all about."

Frannie grinned at her sister-in-law. "Oh, by the way, happy birthday."

"Thanks. Couldn't have a better one."

Frannie pointed toward a small island. "Is that a snake? Swimming away from that island?"

"Looks like it. We nicknamed that 'Snake Island' because there always seem to be some around there."

Frannie shuddered. "Ew. I hate snakes."

"Relax. They're usually quite small. Even if they

swim toward shore, we almost never see them in the campsites."

"Almost?"

"Almost. I didn't realize you were afraid of snakes."

Frannie grimaced. "Mice and bats, too."

Jane Ann laughed. "Maybe camping isn't for you! Just kidding—I really wish you would come more often. Otherwise I'll only have Mickey to talk to after the girls leave home."

"Oh, sure—play on my sympathy." Frannie grinned.

Jane Ann sat forward and pointed toward the end of the lake nearest them. "Is that the girls? Sally and Mona?"

They both peered toward a group thrashing about in the woods on the lakeshore.

"I think so." Frannie opened her mystery and immersed herself in the perils of the family being chased in the woods by a madman.

Various teams of scavengers appeared just often enough to provide diversion; no sign of any serial killers. Otherwise Frannie alternately read and carried on a lazy conversation with Jane Ann. The scavengers returned to report that a team of sixth graders had won and 'probably cheated.' Then they rushed off to get fishing gear.

Jane Ann levered herself out of her chair. "I think we need to do something more active. How about a game of dominos?"

"I don't know how to play," Frannie said.

"Time to learn." Jane Ann grabbed her sister-in-law's hand to pull her up. "C'mon. It's my birthday. You have to play."

They played games at the picnic table, joined by their husbands, for more than two hours. The kids occasionally reported back on the progress in the fishing contest.

Finally Mickey got up from the table. "I'd better get a fire started for supper."

Frannie stood up and stretched. Mickey rummaged in a box for kindling. "I haven't made much progress on those essays I brought along to grade, but it's been a great day."

The reality of school hit Frannie like a box of textbooks. "I haven't thought about school once today."

Mickey clapped her on the shoulder. "Good job! That's the point of all this."

"I'll get the table set," Jane Ann said.

"You sit still," Frannie told her. "You're the birthday girl."

"I've got bean salad in the pop-up and some rolls to warm up," Jane Ann protested.

"The kids will help." Frannie nodded toward the returning teens, who were all talking at once. "Hey, you guys—shut up a minute. I need your help to get supper on because Jane Ann is the queen today. Your dads are cooking steaks and we're going to take care of the rest. Get cleaned up and report back here."

Sam saluted. "Yes, ma'am." He pulled his arm from

behind his back. "But what about these?" He held up two fish on a stringer.

"Sam, that's great! Did you win?"

"No, got second."

Larry said, "Good job, son. How about if I clean'em and we'll have Uncle Mickey throw them on the grill."

"Surf and Turf!" Mickey gave him a thumbs up.

"I've already named 'em. I want to keep them as pets." Sam grinned, but handed them over to Mickey.

Sally ran her fingers through her hair. "I need to shower."

Frannie shook her head. "After supper. It will only be us at the table and we don't care what you look like — we love you anyway. Go wash your hands, and I'll put you and Justine in charge of the rolls and salad that Jane Ann brought."

She kept the kids busy and moving for the next hour. By the time Mickey put the steaks on, the table was set with festive colors and the side dishes were ready.

At the store that morning, Frannie had picked up potato salad to keep things simple. She felt a little guilty that she hadn't made it at home, but knew Jane Ann understood about her last week of school. Besides, if she had brought it along, the raccoons would be the ones enjoying it.

Larry and Sally disappeared into the tent after he whispered instructions to Frannie to keep Jane Ann away. It wasn't easy.

Mona had made her mother a paper crown that said

'Birthday Girl' and placed it crookedly on Jane Ann's head. Jane Ann played the part of the reigning queen expertly and gave orders from her lounge chair to fetch her cheese and crackers or turn up the radio.

She sat up and looked around. "Where's Larry?"

Frannie put down the basket of rolls. "I don't know. Why?"

"I think he should fix his sister a margarita. It's one of the few things he does well." She smirked.

"I don't think he brought the fixings."

"We did. Mickey knows where everything is."

"Can't Mickey fix you one?"

Jane Ann stuck out her tongue. "Not as good as Larry's." A burst of laughter came from the tent. "Oh, that's where he is!"

"Well, he's busy. I'll fix you a drink since you're being such a princess." Frannie laughed.

"Queen. I'm the birthday queen."

Fortunately, Larry and Sally emerged from the tent and Jane Ann called out to him. "Larrry! Come fix a margarita for your beautiful sister!"

"Aren't you carrying this birthday thing a little too far?" But he obliged with a smile.

Another beautiful evening provided ambience for the birthday dinner. Afterward, Larry and Sally produced the birthday cake, such as it was. The layers of unwrapped Twinkies and cupcakes teetered precariously, topped by a dozen blazing candles.

The group's rendition of "Happy Birthday"

compensated for a lack of quality with plenty of decibels. Nearby campers cheered and called out greetings.

Jane Ann took a deep breath and blew. The candles went out, sparked, and blazed anew.

"Oh, no!" Jane Ann laughed. "That old joke again? You guys aren't very original." But she blew on them again, with the same result. Laughing the whole time, she pinched each one out individually. Her girls clapped her on the back.

"Buck up, there, Mom! Don't keel over on us now, just cuz you're a lot older," Justine said.

"Thank you so much. Just for that, you're on the dishwashing detail."

Justine started to groan, but Mickey caught her eye. "Okay."

"Love that enthusiasm," Jane Ann said.

By the time supper was cleared away and the men built up the fire, a glorious sunset was building in the west and reflecting off the lake.

Frannie swirled her wine in the plastic cup, and gazed at the sight.

"That takes my breath away."

Mickey glanced at the sky as he added wood to the fire. "Not to put a damper on things, but that buildup of clouds that is so gorgeous right now is a storm coming in."

"A damper?" Frannie said. "Bad pun, Mick."

"Then get your head out of the clouds."

AFTER THEY DIGESTED DINNER, they made s'mores—this time with graham crackers—sang silly songs, and laughed at Mickey's stories of his early teaching years.

Frannie decided she could get used to such perfect evenings. The firelight reflected in the faces around the fire and she didn't hear one complaint from any of the teenagers.

The only downer was when the ranger stopped by. "Evening, folks! Looks like a great fire."

They all agreed and looked at him expectantly.

"I just wanted to tell everyone that we have a thunderstorm and tornado watch out this evening, so stay alert. If we get a tornado warning, we'll sound a siren and then you should get up to the shower house."

"Thanks," Larry said. "We'll do that."

Frannie looked up at the sky. It was full dark and all of the stars had disappeared. The clouds had moved in. "What do you think, Mickey? Have you been in a bad storm before when you were camping?"

"A couple. The wind is the main thing—if it gets too strong, we should move to the shower house anyway, even if there's no warning. But you know the weather guys. They prefer to err on the side of caution, which is good I guess. We may not get anything."

Frannie nodded and the hilarity resumed around the fire. Before long, even a bumpy air mattress on the ground sounded good.

CHAPTER FOUR

FRANNIE WOKE UP to the crash of thunder, accompanied by lightening that made the tent walls flash and glow. The tent pulled at the stakes and swayed in the wind — like it was trying to rip itself from the ground. She reached out for her watch and glasses that she had laid next to the air mattress and snatched her hand back as she touched cold water.

"Larry!" She could hear the others stirring. She searched for her moccasins as the tent filled with the sounds of everyone shouting over the roar of the wind.

Sam yelled, "Dad! We've got water everywhere!"

They crashed into each other, confused in the dark and frightened by the storm.

"Get to the truck!" Larry yelled.

"What about the sleeping bags and clothes?" Sally yelled back.

"Leave 'em! We won't need 'em if we're struck by lightning."

Sam struggled with the door zipper and Frannie bent to help him. Trent found a small flashlight to give them a little light.

"It's stuck," Sam said. "I can't get it to move either way."

Larry said, "Get out of the way!" When they did, he

launched a kick at the bottom of the door, ripping the canvas. "Now go!"

They tumbled over each other and emerged from the tent into driving rain. Larry reached the truck first, got it unlocked and the rest piled into the cab.

Frannie used the bottom of her wet pajama top to mop her face. Sally and the boys all crammed into the back seat..

"There's some extra blankets back here!" Sally handed a couple forward.

Larry started the engine and turned on their headlights, which were aimed toward their tent. He leaned over the steering wheel and peered through the onslaught toward Ferraros' popup. It rocked and swayed in the wind.

"I can't tell if they're still in there. I wonder if we should go up to the bath house? I didn't hear the siren go off so I don't know how bad it's supposed to get."

Frannie huddled in her blanket. "Doesn't seem like it could get any worse."

"Tornado," Sam said.

"Thanks, Sam—that's encouraging."

"Just sayin'."

"It hasn't been typical tornado weather," Larry said.

"Maybe not typical, but there's such a thing as freak storms. What time is it?"

"Three-thirty," said Trent.

"Maybe there's an all-night diner nearby, and we could get breakfast," Sam said, hopefully.

"Nice try," Frannie said. "Ack! There goes the tent!"

They watched, frozen, as the wind lifted the canvas structure and threw it into Ferraro's popup. It wrapped around one of the drop-down beds, causing the popup to tilt and then settle precariously back on its wheels.

"Wow!" Trent said. "That's not good."

Larry grabbed a stocking hat out of the side pocket in his door. "Sam! Let's go see if we can drag that thing back here. I just hope it didn't damage their camper."

He pushed open his door, letting in a blast of wind and rain. Sam groaned but followed his father. As they leaned into the wind and slogged toward the camper, Trent sighed and said "I'd better help."

Frannie opened her door. "We all should."

When they got to the camper, they could hear voices inside it. Larry and Sam tried to unhook the tent poles from the camper screens. As Frannie and Sally got there, the door opened a crack and Mickey stuck his head out.

"What just happened?"

Frannie yelled above the sound of the wind. "Our tent blew into your camper!" Rain streamed down her face and she shivered in her wet pajamas.

Mickey stared at her. "Good Lord—get in here!"

"No, we have to get it secured. All of our stuff is still in there!"

Mickey slammed the door shut, and Frannie joined the others pulling at the unwieldy wet canvas. Soon Mickey was back out, followed by Jane Ann—both in rain gear. Frannie kicked herself for not even packing a jacket.

Mickey pushed her aside, and Jane Ann grabbed her arm. "Let's find you some dry clothes."

Frannie stood her ground. "We need to save this tent. All of our stuff is in there."

"Well, come with me just a minute." She dragged Frannie up the steps. Inside, she pulled a garbage bag out of a large box and made a couple of snips with a scissors.

Frannie protested the whole time. "What about the others?"

"I have more bags. At least you won't get any wetter. Send someone else in." She pushed Frannie toward the door.

"You sure are bossy," Frannie muttered, and then stumbled down the steps. She returned to the tent project and sent Sally and Trent for the makeshift rain gear.

The group had managed to remove the tent from the camper. With the tent gone, even in the dark, Frannie could see a large hole in the canvas of the popup.

They dragged the heavy tent to the side of their truck out of the wind. Sam and Trent found the door and started handing out bags of clothes and sleeping gear. Everything was wet. Frannie and Sally piled it in the back of the pickup, creating a sodden, stinky mess.

"What d'ya wanna do with the tent?" Mickey yelled.

"Leave it—I'll throw some firewood on it so it doesn't blow any farther," Larry shouted back.

"Unless there's a tornado," Sam said.

"In that case, it won't matter. Get back in the truck. I'll help Mickey fold up the damaged end of their camper so they don't get any more water in."

Sam didn't argue, and they climbed back in the truck.

For a few minutes the quiet was broken only by the sound of the rain as they caught their breath.

Then Sally said, "Is it my imagination or is it letting up a little?"

Frannie listened. "I think you're right." In a matter of minutes, the rain was down to a sprinkle. The relative silence almost hurt Frannie's ears. A lone security light on the other side of the campground silhouetted some of the other campers scurrying around trying to rescue awnings and lawn chairs.

Mickey and Larry gazed up at the still-dark sky, and Mickey slapped Larry on the back with a grin. They talked a minute more, and Larry headed back to the truck.

"We have a plan. We'll go up to the bath house and get hot showers and hopefully find some dry clothes in that mess." He indicated the back of the truck. "Then we'll take Sam's advice and all go to that truck stop on the interstate for some breakfast."

"Yes!" Frannie said. Four solid walls, comfortable seats, and hot food sounded like heaven.

FRANNIE AND SALLY emerged from the women's side of the shower house as dawn began to lighten the sky. Larry and the boys were waiting by the truck so they both stopped on the walk and posed as if they were in a fashion show.

Frannie wore green and blue plaid shorts and an orange-flowered long sleeved shirt—the only items left in her bag that were even close to dry. Red flip flops and a purple bandana completed the outfit.

Sally had found a pair of slightly damp Indian print pajamas and a yellow tee shirt with the logo of a local feed store. Still giggling, they stashed their bags in the back of the truck and climbed into it.

"We are ready for dining out!" Sally announced. She looked at her brother and Trent and started laughing again. "I think I look better than you two."

Sam sported brown and orange flannel pajama bottoms and a Cubs tee shirt, which looked reasonably dry. Trent's sweatshirt was obviously quite wet.

"Trent," Frannie said, "you need something drier to put on. Larry, do you have anything better?"

Larry glanced down at his tee shirt, once dark green, now a drab gray-beige and riddled with holes. Frannie had hidden it in the trash several times but he always managed to find it.

Now he looked at her. "You don't look so great yourself, you know."

"I mean, for Trent! His shirt looks sopping wet."

"Oh, yeah. I think there's another tee shirt in my bag. I'll get it."

THEY FILED INTO THE RESTAURANT. The few patrons appeared to be truckers, most sitting alone. Several gave them suspicious glances as the group slid into a large corner booth.

Sam caught the looks they were getting. "They don't have a dress code here, do they?"

"Doesn't look like it." Mickey said.

As they perused the menus, Larry cleared his throat. "I imagine it's obvious that we will head home this morning."

"Awww, Dad," Sally said.

"That tent is done for," Larry told her. "We don't have any more dry clothes, the raccoons got most of our food yesterday."

"I know. It's just that yesterday was so much fun."

"It was a neat day," Sam said.

Larry and Frannie both looked at him in wonder, not used to hearing too many positive statements from him. Even Trent wagged his head in agreement.

"Brian and Greg invited Mona and Justine and I to go on a picnic this noon," Sally continued, the beginnings of a whine edging her voice.

"Me," Frannie said.

Sally's mouth dropped. "Mom! We don't need a chaperone!"

"No, I mean Mona and Justine and me, not I."

"You're not still my teacher," Sally said.

"No, and I don't teach English, but that doesn't mean you can't use it correctly."

"Aunt Frannie!" Justine said. "Sally can stay with us, can't she?"

Frannie raised her eyebrows and looked at Jane Ann.

"Fine with me. The three of them will have to share a

bed—I'm not giving up mine." Jane Ann grinned. "We'll have to do some duck tape repairs on that end or you'll be sharing the bed with the raccoons."

"Oh, man," Sam said. "She always gets to do the cool stuff."

"It's always best to end something when you still want more rather than when you're tired of it. You'll have much better memories," Frannie said.

Sam looked at her in disbelief. "Who thought that up? Anyway, does that mean you don't want Sally to have good memories?"

In the end, Sam and Trent decided that if they went home they could take in the pool party that night. And maybe certain girls would be there.

As Mickey mopped up some egg yolk with his toast, he said "So, Shoemaker, are you ready to join us on our next trip? We're going to Jackson Lake for five days in about three weeks."

Larry looked at him, speechless for a moment. "Are you crazy? We don't have a tent any more. Our sleeping bags are probably ruined. We've had no sleep..."

Mickey held up his hands. "Relax. You just need a better unit. The only damage we had was from your tent. I'm not blaming you, ya' understand, but did you look around the campground before we left? People in trailers and motorhomes were fine."

"So after this fiasco, we should go spend a fortune on a motorhome?"

"Naw, you could pick up a used trailer or fifth wheel pretty cheap."

"Define cheap."

"Boys, boys," Jane Ann said. "Don't fight. The children are listening."

Sally grinned. "This is the best part."

"Well, there's nothing to fight about," Larry said, returning to his waffle-and-sausage skillet. "We are *not* buying a camper."

CHAPTER FIVE

A WEEK LATER, Mickey called and invited them to go to an RV show in a nearby town. Larry balked.

"We're really not interested in buying a camper, Mick."

"We just go for the looking. There's entertainment and cooking demonstrations—it's just a fun day. Whaddya have to lose?"

"My sanity. Every time I hang around you."

Frannie walked into the living room just as Larry hung up.

"Who was that?"

He grinned. "My girlfriend."

"And she's affecting your sanity? Are you sure it wasn't Mickey?"

"You got me. They want us to go to an RV show Saturday."

She shrugged. "We have nothing else on."

"We aren't buying a camper."

"I get that."

SO THEY WENT. They enjoyed barbecue sandwiches and watched a demonstration on cast-iron cooking. They trudged up and down steps into new travel trailers, fifth-wheel trailers, Class Cs with sleeping quarters over the truck cab, Class B vans, and giant Class A motorhomes.

They all smelled like new cars and had clear plastic over the upholstery and mattresses. Frannie thought most didn't look like they belonged in a campground. Some seemed too plush for trips in them to be called camping, and others didn't seem like very practical arrangements.

Many had price tags higher than Frannie and Larry's house had twenty years earlier. Still, there was something about them that beckoned to Frannie: cozy, efficient, and —most important— protection from storms.

On the way home, Jane Ann and Mickey discussed the fine points of several trailers and Class Cs that they admired.

"Why would you buy something you have to hook up? Seems like the ones you can drive would be a lot easier," Frannie said.

"For one thing, they're more expensive because you're buying an engine, too. And you either have to tow a car or stay put. No trips to the grocery store," Mickey said. "But you're right—they are easier. That's why we're looking at Class Cs."

"Those are the ones with the bed over the cab, right?" Frannie asked. "I understand why you wouldn't want to do that with one of those huge bus-like things, but it seems like the Class Cs wouldn't be that hard to take to a grocery store."

Jane Ann shook her head. "They aren't if there's a big

parking lot. But first you have to unhook power and water and stow everything so that nothing rolls around while you're driving. Then when you get back, hook power and water back up and get everything out again. It's a lot of hassle."

Frannie leaned back in her seat. "Boy, lot to think about."

Mickey said, "Well, Shoemaker—you're pretty quiet. See anything you liked?"

"We aren't buying a camper."

"Yeah, I know, but if someone was going to give you one, which one would you take?"

Larry narrowed his eyes and glanced over at Mickey. "Are you buying me a camper, Mick?"

"Of course not."

"Then what's the point?"

"Geesh, what a grouch. You're right—you don't deserve a camper. You'd just deposit your bad vibes in it and then you'd never be able to sell it."

Larry grinned. "Right."

A COUPLE OF WEEKS LATER, the Shoemakers were about to sit down to supper on their deck, when a raucous horn sounded in the alley. A light blue pickup came into view pulling a white and blue travel trailer.

"Who is that?" Larry asked.

The driver's window slid down and Mickey's head popped out. "Hey, campers!" he yelled.

Larry dropped his napkin by his plate and got up.

"He doesn't give up, does he?" But he was smiling.

Frannie and the kids followed him to the alley.

Mickey jumped out of the truck and held up both arms. "Surprise!"

"This is for us?" Larry said.

"Of course not. You don't deserve it. We do. Sorry, Frannie, kids, but he's the Grinch that Stole Summer. Want to check it out?"

Jane Ann was already leading them back to the camper door, while Larry said, "New wheels too? Pretty snazzy." He and Mickey hung back and discussed the merits of the new truck while Jane Ann led the tour of the trailer.

The outside of the trailer was white with graphic stripes in two shades of blue. Inside, Jane Ann proudly pointed out the neat cabinets and the dining table and couch that made into beds. At one end, a folding door led to a bedroom with a double mattress, and at the other end two bunks fit into one corner and a bathroom in the other. White walls set off the blue curtains and upholstery.

Jane Ann's tone was a little apologetic. "This actually sleeps eight, but I think the beds out here would be a little too cozy,"

Frannie grinned. "Well, it's beautiful, Jane Ann. I'm so happy for you. What did you do with your pop-up?"

Jane Ann started out the door. "Mickey's going to put it up for sale." She turned around. "Do you guys want it?"

Frannie shook her head. "Larry says we're not buying a camper."

Sally heard this exchange. "Mom! We should! That would be so cool!"

"Talk to your dad," Frannie said, but her voice said, *Don't get your hopes up.*

Sally attacked him the minute they got out the door. "Daddy! We should buy their old one!"

Larry smiled at her but shook his head. "We're not looking for a camper."

OVER THE NEXT FEW DAYS, Sam and Sally brought up the topic of the pop-up until Larry began to get testy about it. He made it clear that after their Memorial Day experience, he didn't consider the popup much more protection than the tent.

Jane Ann reported back after their first outing that the new trailer was a "dream" and everyone enjoyed the added space.

Frannie was pleased for them, and a little envious.

The next week, Larry planned to drop off his truck after work for an oil change and asked Frannie to follow him to the dealer. When she arrived at the police station, he was finishing up some paper work.

"I'll just be a minute. Do you want to wait in the break room?"

The converted office contained a small table, two folding chairs, a disreputable-looking coffee pot and a small, ancient pink refrigerator. It didn't even have a separate freezer. The rounded door was camouflaged with policy notices, upcoming events (that had passed some time ago), and items for sale.

Frannie opened the fridge to check the soda selection. As she closed the door, she glanced over the offerings, thinking that in several hundred years, that door would offer some archeologist several years of study.

Then her eyes stopped on one sale notice. Someone had a used camper that looked pretty good in the grainy photo. The price was much less than anything at the RV show.

Larry stuck his head in the door. "Ready to go?"

"Sure. Did you see this?" She pointed at the sheet of paper.

"No—I rarely come in here. What is it?"

She took it off the fridge and showed him. "This is very reasonable, it's only five years old, and says it's been gently used. Maybe we could do something like this?"

He read the ad and then looked at her. "Are you seriously interested in this? I didn't think you ever wanted to camp."

She screwed up her face. "It was a good time. Well, except for the storm. And the raccoons. The kids loved it."

"But how about you? Did you love it?"

She thought a moment. "I did. It was so relaxing. Mostly."

Larry looked at the ad again. "I guess it wouldn't hurt to look at it. I don't recognize the name so I don't know who posted this. Hard to tell how long it's been here. I'll find out."

THE OWNER OF THE CAMPER lived in the town of Norton about twenty miles from Perfection Falls. Glen Hansen was a ruddy-faced man with large hands, obviously used to the outdoors. He led them to a large parking pad behind his garage. Larry and Frannie looked at each other, confused. A big new Winnebago motorhome sat there.

Hansen continued around the motorhome and pointed at a much smaller, well-used trailer crouched in the shadows. Hansen took off his cap and wiped his forehead. "We used it a lot. But we've retired now and are selling our house. We're going to live in this baby full-time." He patted the front of the motorhome proudly. "Going to see all of the sights there are to see in this big beautiful country."

"That sounds wonderful," Frannie said, although she didn't think that much camping would be for her. "We aren't sure if we really want to camp, but we're thinking about it. We have two teenage kids who enjoy it and are pressuring us." She gave him a little smile.

Hansen turned to her.

"Ma'am, if you have teenagers who actually want to go camping and spend time with you, you'd better arrange it somehow. Whether you buy this camper, or a tent, or a fifty-foot motor home — whatever it takes. You want to see the inside?"

"We'd love to," Frannie said, and Larry agreed.

Hansen led the way up two shallow steps.

"How long is this?" Larry asked.

Frannie thought he was probably trying to appear knowledgeable about camper buying.

"Twenty-seven feet." He pointed where a bed filled one end under a cozy curved ceiling. He nodded toward bright turquoise and green curtains. "My wife made all of the curtains."

The other end held a dinette and booth. In the center a small kitchen sat across from a couch. "The dinette and couch each make into a bed."

Frannie thought of Mickey and Jane Ann's new trailer with the separate bedroom and bunk room. But this would make more sense for them until they decided how serious they were about it.

Hansen opened a narrow door next to the refrigerator. Smaller than any closet, the tiny space housed a toilet and sink. "It doesn't have a shower. We always used the ones in the campgrounds."

Larry shrugged. "That's doable, I guess. It's what we did with a tent."

Hansen showed them the location of the water heater and pump, and the little furnace. He explained about propane and the refrigerator. Frannie half listened as she opened cabinets and storage compartments. Hansen, or someone, had cleaned them thoroughly.

On the way home, they talked about the little camper.

Larry said, "Well, at the price he's asking, I would

think we could always get our money out of it if we don't like it."

Frannie concealed her surprise at his receptiveness and tried to sound reluctant. "I suppose that's true."

FOR THE NEXT WEEK, they discussed it off and on. In the end, they decided to offer Glenn Hansen his asking price for the trailer. They told Sam and Sally, called Hansen, and all piled in the truck to go pick it up. Larry had bought a hitch and had it installed before the eventful day.

"Is there room for Sam and me to bring a friend?" Sally asked, when they were on their way.

"Well, the beds aren't very big, but we could always take a small tent."

In spite of the small size, the kids were excited as they explored the nooks and crannies. Hansen gave Frannie and Larry a thorough primer on the fundamentals of the workings, maintenance, and towing of the little trailer. They got it home and backed into their driveway without incident.

"So, when are we going camping?" Sam asked.

"Relax," Frannie said. "We're going with Uncle Mickey and Aunt Jane Ann next week. Before that, I need to pack it with all of the basic stuff."

"Basic stuff? Like what?"

"You know—silly stuff like dishes, pots and pans, food, bedding..."

"Oh. Yeah, I guess you need that."
"We need that."
"Whatever."

CHAPTER SIX

BY THE NEXT THURSDAY, Frannie had the cupboards and refrigerator stuffed with everything she could think of — possibly a little beyond the basics.

The forecast was all over the weather map, so to speak, and after packing several pair of her shorts and tees neatly in one cupboard above the bed, she crammed in two pair of jeans and three sweatshirts. Heavy socks could be stuffed in the corners.

Frannie assigned the kids each a cupboard, but when she checked to see if they were adequately prepared, a Walkman and several sports magazines fell out of Sam's cupboard with no sign of clothes. Sally had enough makeup in hers for a movie set.

"Kids," she said, when she returned to the house, "you need to get some clothes out there. A cold front is supposed to come through Saturday night so you need to take a few warm weather things. Also jeans and sweatshirts."

"I thought we had a furnace in that thing," Sally said.

"We do, but you're not going to sit inside all weekend, are you?"

"Um, no?"

"Right answer."

Food was another issue. Mickey and Jane Ann would be with them and Mickey was always prepared for any culinary emergency. But if she and Larry were going to camp on an ongoing basis, they couldn't always depend on the Ferraros to provide a full pantry.

Between phone calls with Jane Ann, she came up with menus for three main meals that she thought were doable. By the time she loaded the necessary ingredients in the little fridge, there was barely space for sandwich makings, eggs, and sausage. And she had no milk or other beverages in there. Those would just have to go in coolers. Even so, she had to push much of the food into the fridge and close the door with force.

On it went. When they had looked at the units at the RV show, and even at this smaller trailer at Glen Hanson's farm, it appeared that, compared to the old tent, space would be no problem. But it was.

Every category of equipment was a decision. How many pans and what kind to put in? How many dishes? What could they get by on in cleaning supplies? She smiled at her fretting. They weren't life-or-death questions. They would not be camping anytime soon in the Alaskan bush or along the Amazon. But still, it didn't hurt to be prepared.

Larry assembled a small tool kit and filled two big plastic totes with firewood. He stowed fishing gear and grill utensils in one of the outside compartments. He drained the antifreeze that had been in the trailer through the winter and flushed out the water system as Glen

Hansen had directed. When he went to put his clothes in the cupboard that Frannie had reserved for him, he found a stack of VCR tapes including *The Lion King* and *Dumb and Dumber*.

"Sal!" he called when he entered the house, tapes in hand. "What are these doing in the camper?"

"Welll, I thought if it rains…"

"We don't have a TV or a VCR player in there."

"Maybe we should get one before we go." She smiled.

"And maybe not. Find some games and a book. And put them in your cupboard."

"I was going to, but there's no room."

"And how do we solve that problem, my dear?"

"Um, assign me an extra cupboard?" She batted her eyes at her father.

He swatted her gently on the behind. "You're not too old to spank. Get out there and reorganize your stuff."

When the time came to leave, Frannie felt she had half her life crammed in the little trailer, but still worried that she was forgetting something.

LARRY HAD ARRANGED Friday as a day of vacation and wasn't on call for the weekend, so Frannie looked forward to a few days away from the phone. Larry had started carrying a cell phone but kept it switched off when he wasn't on call. The whole family was ready to go by nine A.M.

As Larry finished his breakfast, he said to Frannie, "I'll load the kids' bikes and the lawn chairs in the pickup. The next challenge will be hooking up the trailer. Are you ready to direct me?"

Frannie was confused. "Direct you?"

"Help me line up the truck to get the hitch in the right place."

"Um, sure." At least she hoped she could. She had been concentrating on everything they needed to do to camp, but hadn't even thought about getting the trailer to the campground. How hard could it be? Thousands of people did it.

"Do you have everything loaded that you want to take?" Larry asked.

"As much as will fit. Oh, wait, I have a bowl of Jello salad I made last night to put in the fridge. Then I'm done."

"Okay. I'll be ready when you are."

After clearing the breakfast makings, she took a bowl of lime Jello with pears out of the house refrigerator and covered it with plastic wrap. She had already used all of her plastic bowls with lids for other food. When she took it out to the camper refrigerator, she could see that things would need to be rearranged to get the bowl in. She had just finished some creative cramming when Larry poked his head in the door.

"Ready?"

"Sure." She let the fridge door swing shut, took a quick look around, and grabbed her set of camper keys off the counter. "Shall I lock the door and put the steps away?" she called to Larry once she was outside.

"Go ahead."

She locked the door after only three tries and carefully folded up the metal steps, feeling pretty pleased with herself for completing this much of the process.

"Stand right over here." Larry directed her to a spot near the hitch where he could see her in his driver's side mirror. "If you can just let me know whether I'm going straight or not and how far I have to go, that'll be great."

She nodded and waited for him to get in and start the truck. Then she started motioning him back with her left hand while keeping an eye on the two hitches.

So far, so good. Not until he was too close did she realize that the trailer tongue was not raised up enough for the ball on the truck hitch to go under it. The hitch hit the tongue with a resounding clang at the same time that she threw up her right hand in a "Stop!" motion.

Larry pulled forward a couple of feet and stuck his head out the window. "Which is it?"

Frannie looked up. "Which is what?"

"Your hands. You're motioning me forward with one hand and telling me to stop with the other."

She looked at her hands, still in the air. "Oh." She tucked them both behind her back. "Sorry."

He opened the door and swung out of the truck to inspect the problem. "The tongue isn't high enough." He showed her how to crank the jack to raise the tongue. "Now, one direction at a time, okay?" His tone said his patience would not last long.

Sam and Sally were watching the operation. "Want

me to try it, Dad?" Sam asked.

"No, she'll be fine." Frannie could have sworn she heard him add "I hope" as he got back into the truck.

This time she kept her right hand down, and Larry edged the truck more slowly, but he was too far to the right. She ran up to his window.

"You're about this much too far to the right." She tried to show the distance with her index finger and thumb.

"My right?"

She thought a moment. "Yeah—my right, your right, same thing."

He huffed. She didn't know what that meant, but he said, "I'll try it again." She backed up, and he pulled forward a few feet. She went back to her post and the maneuver, report, and retry routine was repeated three more times before she jubilantly threw up both hands and yelled "Score!"

"I think you mean touchdown, Mom," Sam said.

"Who cares? We did it!" She moved out of the way so Larry could crank the tongue back down over the hitch.

Larry connected chains and plugged in cords. Once satisfied that nothing dragged on the ground, he stood up and put his hands on his hips. "I think that's it. Everybody get in the truck."

They did, and headed over to the Ferraros. The park was about a two-hour drive and the Shoemakers would follow Mickey and Jane Ann.

As they pulled up, Mickey looked up from his own

hookup process, and started to laugh and point.

Larry got out of the truck "What's your problem, Ferraro?"

Mickey continued to point at the back of the trailer. "Did you forget to unplug?"

Frannie got out and joined her husband as he looked back in dismay and the heavy electrical cord trailing in the street from the back of the trailer. He ran his hand over his crewcut and turned to Frannie. "You know what else? We didn't take the wheel chocks out and must have driven over them. I thought it was pulling hard as we came out of the driveway."

"What do we do?" Frannie said.

Mickey had joined them. "I've got extra blocks of wood we can use for your wheels. Check your cord and make sure it's okay." Mickey grinned. "And you might want to stow the cord rather than dragging it along behind."

"What would I do with out you, Mick? Other than be a much happier man?" Larry went to check the cord, called back "Looks okay," and coiled it in its compartment.

Frannie and Larry got back in the truck to wait for Mickey to pull out ahead of them. They looked at each other.

Larry said, "Is this really stupid or what?"

At the same time, Frannie said, "Why did we decide to do this?"

They both started to laugh and couldn't stop.

TO THEIR IMMENSE RELIEF, the journey to the park was uneventful. No strong wind whipped them around. Although the clouds hung low, the rain stayed away.

When they reached the park, Mickey led them first to a fresh water spigot. He had warned them that there were no water hookups at the site so they would need to fill their tank before they set up.

They didn't have reserved sites on this trip, so when the water tanks were full, they drove slowly around the campground looking for two good sites together. They stopped several times to check obstacles and the levelness of a site. The second time around, Mickey and Larry agreed on two adjoining spots with a nice campfire area.

Frannie got out to help Larry park. The process went more smoothly than the hookup had. However, when they checked the levels on the camper, they had a slight tilt to one side, so Larry got a board out of the truck that he had brought just for this purpose. He pulled the camper forward a few feet, had Sally move the board into position behind the camper tires on the low side, and in only two tries got it backed up on the board. It still wasn't perfectly level, but much better. They unhooked the truck, and Sam cranked the jacks down that supported each corner.

Frannie opened the steps and unlocked the door. "Get out those lawn chairs, Larry. I'm ready to kick back with a cool drink."

She stepped inside the camper. The squish beneath

her foot signaled the mess she saw all over the floor. The refrigerator door stood open, and a dozen broken eggs mixed with the lime Jello to create an abstract design on the vinyl floor.

"Oh no!"

"What?" Sally ran to the door to survey the destruction.. "Omigosh!"

Jane Ann heard the fuss and left the tablecloth that she was spreading on the picnic table. "What happened?" Her mouth dropped open, and then she started to laugh. She noticed Frannie's crestfallen face and put her arm around her sister-in-law's shoulders.

"I'll get some paper towels and help you clean it up. Too bad we didn't bring a shop vac."

Frannie sunk down on the picnic table bench and put her head in her hands. Larry poked his head in. "What's wrong? Oh! I see."

"Jane Ann went to get paper towels. Of course I forgot to bring any. I don't think we were meant to do this."

"We'll all help with the cleanup." It was the type of consoling suggestion Larry often made, which Frannie deemed well-meant but impractical.

"Thanks, but there isn't room for more than one or two in there."

He cocked his head. "Is that the water pump running?"

"What does the water pump sound like?"

"Like that." He practically leaped up the steps,

tiptoed around the mess and opened the bathroom door.

"Oh, no!"

"Now what?"

"The sink faucet was still on from when I flushed out the system!" He leaned over the counter and pushed a button on the tank indicator. "We're about out of water." He pushed another button. "And our gray water tank is almost full."

Frannie couldn't move her mind past the gooey mess on the floor. "What does that mean? How could we be almost out?"

He sighed. "This bathroom faucet was turned on and apparently so was the pump. After I filled the tank, we drove around, deciding on a site, got parked, set up — the whole time, water was running from the fresh water tank to the gray. So now we need to hook back up and go dump the gray and refill the fresh."

Frannie threw her hands up. "One thing at a time. This mess has to be cleaned up first."

"Yeah. Here comes Jane Ann. I'll get a garbage bag for the paper towels."

Soon they were on hands and knees mopping up.

"This has to be one of the slimiest messes ever," Frannie said. "And disgusting."

Jane Ann paused and sat back on her haunches. "Oh, I don't know. Sometimes in the Operating Room, there's —"

Frannie put her hands over her ears. "La-la-la-la — I don't want to hear it."

They finished sopping up the worst of the mess and Sally hauled the garbage bag to the dumpster. The women went back outside where Larry and Mickey stood by a golf cart, deep in conference with another man.

Frannie walked up to them. "We're as done as we can be without water to finish. So now we need to hook the camper back up?"

She realized that Larry looked more relaxed. "Maybe not. This is George, the campground host. He thinks we can hook up enough hoses to reach that hydrant over there." He pointed to the middle of the next loop. "Since all of the water in our gray water tank is actually fresh, he said I can just dump it on the ground."

George said, "I'll go get a couple more hoses. If you guys each have one, that should do it. Let's get this taken care of." He jumped in the golf cart and sped off.

Frannie could have kissed the man.

Chapter Seven

THE DUMPING AND REFILL of the tanks took almost an hour. The kids went off to explore the area while Frannie and Jane Ann watched the proceedings from lawn chairs. Jane Ann brought out a bag of chips and a container of dip.

"It's probably too early for wine, isn't it?" Frannie said.

Jane Ann laughed. "Maybe we should wait until we get your camper cleaned up and in order. Although it's tempting."

Frannie shook her head. "I don't know. I don't think camping is for us."

"Nonsense! Everyone goes through some beginner's pains."

"But this much? So far we forgot to unplug the cord, close the refrigerator tight, shut off the faucets and pump — and we aren't even set up yet."

"It'll get better. At least it's not raining."

A crack of thunder exploded above them. Large drops of rain plopped around them and on their heads.

Jane Ann jumped up. "Quick—inside!" She grabbed the chips and dip while Frannie folded the lawn chairs and stuck them under the Ferraros' trailer. They ducked inside, wiping raindrops from their faces. Larry and Mickey weren't far behind.

"Where are the kids?" Mickey dried off with a towel Jane Ann gave him.

Jane Ann grimaced. "They went to check things out around the park. I imagine the rain will bring them back pretty quickly."

"I hope so." Frannie peered out the window. "It doesn't seem to be letting up at all."

The drumming on the roof almost made normal conversation impossible. The rain went on and Larry went back and forth to check tanks and hoses. But the kids didn't appear.

"Maybe I should take the truck and look for them," Mickey said.

Jane Ann didn't hesitate. "Good idea!" She grabbed his raincoat off a hook by the door and handed it to him.

He shrugged into the coat. "Aren't you going to try and talk me out of it?"

"No. Get going!"

"I'm sure they're okay," Mickey protested, as she gave him a gentle push out the door.

"Should I go too?" Larry asked.

"No," Jane Ann said. "If you did, there wouldn't be room for all of them to ride back."

Frannie watched out the window as Mickey drove away, and then turned to Larry.

"How are you coming on the setup?"

"The gray water tank is empty and the fresh water is

filling." He looked at his watch. "I need to go back out in about five minutes, rain or no rain. It should be done by then."

By the time he went to check the water, Mickey had not returned, but the rain had started to let up.

"Do you think the kids are okay?" Frannie asked.

Jane Ann was arranging a large bouquet of daisies and lilies that she had brought from home. "What? Oh, sure. They may be awfully wet but I'm sure they're fine."

"I hope so. Is there anything I can do to help you?"

"No, just getting a few things out. These will go on the picnic table when the rain quits. Then we'll go mop up your floor. There's a bucket and some rags in that closet back there. Fill it up with some soap and water here because it will take a while for yours to heat up."

Frannie did as she was told, grateful to have a task that she could complete without screw ups. She hoped. Scrubbing the floor on her hands and knees gave her something to do while she fretted about the kids. What if one of them fell off a trail and was seriously hurt?

Jane Ann went back and forth to get fresh buckets of water and they finished just as the rain quit. Larry announced they now had water, as Mickey pulled back in the campsites with a truckload of teenagers.

The kids piled out, laughing and soaking wet.

Mickey gave a wry grin. "They found a shelter and were pretty dry until I made them come back out in the rain to get in the truck."

SINCE IT WAS A FRIDAY, the campground was filling up. A small fifth-wheel backed into a site across the road from the Ferraros and the Shoemakers. Two children roamed the campsite while the parents set up chairs, a utility table, and a small awning. The boy looked about eight and helped his father string some lights.

The girl was younger with black hair cut short and large dark eyes. She stood at the edge of the road, staring at the Shoemaker campsite, twirling what appeared to be a pair of handcuffs around her fingers. Other than the hand movements, she was as still as a statue.

"Wow." Sally came up behind her mother's lawn chair. "She's kind of spooky."

Frannie looked at her in surprise. Sally always loved children. As the baby of the family, she had wished for a younger sibling.

When she was about three, two Sundays in a row featured an infant baptism in their church service. After the second, Sally wanted to know if they could take the baby home. Something about the ritual of passing the baby from parents to minister and back again, everyone looking at the baby, touching it on the head, and passing the baby around after the service, made Sally think that church was sort of like a pet store for babies.

"Maybe she's just kind of lonesome," Frannie said. But she shuddered a little as the girl just continued to stare in their direction, not really focused on anything.

"You're right. I'll go talk to her."

Sally wandered across the road. "Hi! My name's Sally.

70

Is this your first camping trip?"

The girl continued to stare into the distance and spin the handcuffs.

Sally persisted. "What's your name?"

Nothing.

The mother looked up and saw Sally. "Lyssa! Come here."

Sally got the message, said, "See you later," and returned to her own campsite. As she did, the mother walked over, put her hands on the girl's shoulders, turned her around, and marched her back to the camper.

"What do you think? She never even looked at me," Sally said to Frannie.

"Either she will take a little while to come around and speak to you, or she has a problem that you can't fix."

"What do you mean?"

Frannie shook her head. "Could be a lot of things. Some kind of disability — or maybe just very shy."

They didn't see any more of the family across the way that evening. They sat around the crackling fire, full and satisfied, after cleaning up the supper of hot dogs and hamburgers. The rain was done and the stars sparkled.

Frannie reflected that maybe camping was like childbirth. You had to go through a lot of pain to get to the pleasant moments like this. Was it worth it? Maybe.

SATURDAY MORNING DAWNED warm and still, with a promise of heat to come. Frannie rose first and drank in the sun creeping through the trees along with her fragrant coffee. She loved early mornings.

A slightly disreputable-looking green pickup with a topper over the back sat at the end of the road tucked into a site against the trees. It hadn't been there when they went to bed so it must have come in during the night.

As Frannie watched, the door in the back opened and a man of indeterminate age stepped out, looking as scruffy as the truck. He glanced around at the campground and moved a box from the ground behind the truck into the passenger seat. Then he locked the truck and disappeared into the trees.

Frannie waited for him to reappear but gave up and turned her attention to a flock of Canadian geese landing on the lake.

The kids had wanted to make pancakes, so she supervised Sam while he mixed up the batter in the camper. Food prep in even this tiny kitchen was worlds above using bowls balanced on overturned coolers.

They would do the actual cooking outside, so she sent Sam with the dripping bowl out to Mickey's tutelage. Mickey had a large griddle propped on the fire ring and would instruct Sam in the fine art of pancake flipping.

Sally helped Mona and Justine in the bacon department. Jane Ann had plugged a large electric skillet into an outside outlet on their trailer and placed it on a folding table that the girls could crowd around. From the discussion, it sounded like too many chiefs and not enough Indians.

When the bacon was done, Mickey used the skillet to fry a few eggs. They gathered at the picnic table and concentrated for a few minutes on passing syrup and butter and building towers of cakes, eggs and bacon.

They were really getting down to business when a woman's voice caused them all to look up. "Good morning!" It was the woman from across the road.

"Good morning," Jane Ann said.

The woman focused on Sally. "I just wanted to apologize for scaring you away last night."

"Tha's okay," Sally mumbled, her mouth full of pancake and her tone wary.

"I know you were just being friendly," the woman went on, "so I want to explain. Lyssa is autistic and she's also partially blind from birth."

Sally's face softened, and she wiped her mouth. "Oh! I'm so sorry!"

The woman held up her hands. "Don't be. She's a delightful child. She loves camping because she's fascinated by birds. I won't interrupt your breakfast any more—I just wanted you to know I didn't mean to be rude. It's just—" she paused and gave a little forced laugh, "things can get a little tense when we're setting up, and I'm so worried she'll wander off."

"We know about tension when setting up," Jane assured her.

This time the woman's laugh was genuine. "Thank you. My name is Teri, by the way. Come and visit whenever you see us out." She nodded at Sally.

After she was gone, Sally said, "Now I feel terrible."

Frannie put her arm around her daughter. "Don't. You were just trying to be nice, and there's nothing wrong with that."

Sally forked in a couple more bites of pancake and chewed thoughtfully. Then she brightened. "Maybe I could talk to her about birds."

"Good idea. You *are* kind of a bird-brain," Sam said.

Mona threw a chunk of pancake at him and Frannie glared at both of them. "That's a wonderful idea, Sally."

Jane Ann got up from the table and gave Mona's arm a good-humored tug. "You and Sam are the committee to clear the table and do the dishes."

The mothers had their backs turned when Sally stuck her tongue out at Sam.

"When that's done," Mickey said, "we're going on a family hike. There're great trails here."

Mona and Justine groaned. "We already explored yesterday," Justine said.

Mickey held up a finger. "Ah, but you got caught in the rain. Did you get to the caves?"

"Caves?" Mona asked, and then clapped a hand over her mouth.

Mickey was triumphant. "See? You barely scratched the surface. Get the dishes done and then fill your water bottles and find your scruffiest shoes. We're going spelunking!"

The teenagers exchanged eye-rolls and headed off to do their tasks.

They gathered again around the picnic table twenty minutes later. Mickey had a park map spread on the table and pointed out the trail they were going to take. Sam tweaked Justine's hair and Sally shoved him.

Mickey placed a stubby finger on a point on the map. "We can at least go as far as this cave this morning. Watch out for poison ivy. And bears."

He got Sam's attention. "Bears?"

Jane Ann waved her hand. "He's lying. But there is poison ivy."

As they headed toward the trailhead, Frannie noticed that the family across the road was outside. Lyssa sat in a lawn chair scuffing her heels in the dirt, while her mother worked on a cooking project near the fire. Sally dropped back to Frannie.

"I'm going to stop and say hi, okay? I'll catch up."

"Sure."

Frannie glanced over her shoulder several times to see Sally reach the campsite and talk to the little girl. Lyssa turned her head toward Sally seemingly interested.

A few minutes later, Sally came panting up beside Frannie. "Can I skip the hike? I mentioned birds to her, and I think I made a connection."

Her mother smiled at her. "Absolutely. We'll miss you, but I'll be anxious to hear how it goes when we get back."

Sally dashed off again.

Jane Ann fell in step beside Frannie. "She can't resist a sparrow with a broken wing, can she?"

Frannie shook her head. "Never could."

Sally had gone through the usual career choices as a preteen: figure skater, pet store owner, rock star, and video game designer. After a church mission trip the previous year she decided that she wanted to be a social worker. This goal remained constant for an astonishing eight months.

She had developed a special affinity for small children with disabilities. During the spring, she had volunteered as an aide at the elementary school.

The first section of the trail led downhill toward the river. Some times the sun dappled the ground ahead like an usher's flashlight in a theatre and then ducked behind clouds leaving the path in gloom.

Sam entertained himself by hiding behind trees and jumping out at Mona and Justine.

"Looks like we should have brought someone along for Sam to pal around with," Frannie said. "But we thought for this first trip, we shouldn't subject outsiders."

Jane Ann grinned. "I'm guessing that the girls are egging him on. They *like* to scream."

At the river, the path turned uphill to wind around gullies, along a ridge, and back down into a glen. There they walked along a boardwalk built into the side of the cliff until they reached a large opening.

Frannie opted to wait outside while the others explored the cave. As she sat on a boulder in the shade, she wondered how Sally was succeeding in her friendship attempt with little Lyssa.

CHAPTER EIGHT

SHE NEEDN'T HAVE WORRIED. As they returned to their campsite, soft giggles came from the girl as Sally made animal noises to entertain her. As they began lunch preparations, Sally returned to the group. Her face glowed.

Frannie arranged sandwich makings on the picnic table. "Looks like it went pretty well."

"Lyssa is *so* sweet. She loves birds and knows almost every bird call! She's amazing."

"Does she go to school yet?" Jane Ann asked.

Sally grabbed a handful of potato chips. "Next year. Her mom is pretty nervous about it."

Lunch was the usual chaos, and afterwards they sat at the table discussing plans for the afternoon. The day was heating up and only huge, rolling clouds gave relief from the sun.

Mona pushed her hair back from her face. "I wish they had swimming here."

Her father grinned. "What about an afternoon of tubing? There's a rental place upriver from here."

A chorus of "Cool!" "Yes!" and "Awesome!" from the teenagers greeted that suggestion.

"I kind of had a nap in mind," Larry said.

"You don't have to go," Mickey said. "Stay here and sleep your life away."

They continued to argue while the kids raced to don swimsuits, old tee shirts, and shoes. Frannie found some old shorts and a cast-off cotton shirt of Larry's. Larry stuck with his plan to nap, so Mickey drove with Jane Ann, Frannie, and Sam in the cab. The girls rode in the pickup bed. Mickey said the rental place was only a half mile up a blacktop road from the park.

They had just pulled out on the camp road when Teri, Lyssa's mother, stepped out in front of the truck, waving her arms. She had a panicked look on her face.

Mickey slammed on the brakes, causing the girls in the back end to scream, of course.

He rolled down his window. "What's the trouble?"

"Have you seen Lyssa? Have you seen my little girl?"

Mickey shook his head, and Sally hung over the side of the truck.

"What's happened?"

Teri spotted her and moved toward the back. She wrung her hands and fought back tears.

"I went inside to get her lunch, and decided to put a few things away — so it was probably ten minutes or so — and when I came back out, she was gone!"

Larry had walked over from his lounge chair. "Have you notified the authorities?"

"No, my husband isn't even here. I don't know what to do. Do you know where I could find the ranger?"

Larry led her toward a lawn chair by their trailer. "I'll take care of it. I'm a cop and will get a search going. I've got a cell phone."

Mickey called out the window, "We'll all help look. Sit down girls!" He put the truck in reverse and backed into his own site. Sally was out of the truck the minute it stopped.

"Would she go into the woods, d'ya think?" she asked Teri.

"I don't know—she's never wandered off." The tears came.

Jane Ann patted her on the shoulder. Frannie looked toward the woods and the trail they had followed earlier. Her eye caught the pickup camper that had pulled in during the night. She hoped the scruffy guy wasn't connected to the disappearance, but she hadn't seen him all day.

Sally took charge. "Let's start looking while Dad finds the ranger. Sam and Mona, you guys take your bikes and go around the campground—check all of the sites and don't forget the shower house. Justine, why don't you and Uncle Mickey check the woods on the other side of the campground—there's another trail over there. Aunt Jane Ann, can you stay here with Teri? Mom and I will check that trail we took this morning."

Frannie looked at her daughter in surprised admiration. Larry raised an eyebrow at her as he headed toward his truck. "Just like her mother—bossy."

Sally was ready to go, "C'mon, Mom!"

As they headed toward the trail, Sally lost some of her confidence and worry crept into her voice. "I bet she just wandered off and got confused. I don't think she's used to being on her own."

"Most five-year-olds aren't." They passed the pickup camper, but Frannie saw no sign of Scruffy Guy on the other side either.

On the trail, they began to call Lyssa's name. Frannie scrutinized one side of the trail while Sally inspected the other. They got to the river with no sign of the little girl.

"Did she tell you much?" Frannie asked. "What does she like to do?"

"Mostly she talks about birds." Sally pushed aside a straggly elderberry along the trail and peered beneath it. "She can't see much, but does know colors. So she described birds to me and then mimicked their sounds. Pretty amazing."

Frannie trudged ahead a few minutes and then said, "Did she talk about anything she wanted to do while she was camping?"

"I don't think so."

They continued in silence until they reach the ridge. The Scruffy Guy nagged at Frannie's imagination. She should have told Larry about him, even though there was no reason to suspect him of anything. She caught a glimpse of something silver laying under a dead tree branch.

"Sally! Aren't these the toy handcuffs Lyssa had?"

Sally stopped and turned them over in her hands.

"They must be. They look just like them." She stared at her mother, her earlier confidence replaced by uncertainty and a little fear. "She must have come this way."

"Or someone brought her," Frannie said. She told Sally about the suspicious man. "I hate to accuse someone, but he was acting funny and when a child goes missing—"

"Oh, Mom—I hope not. Should we go back and tell the others that she must have come this way? Get everyone out here looking?"

"I don't know. It's a ways back and I hate to lose the time. Maybe you should go and I'll keep looking—"

"Mom! I just thought of something. She talked about wanting to find a cowbird. There're supposed to be some in this park." She turned and called "Lyssa! "Lyssa! Where are you?" The woods were silent.

"Let's go down to the boardwalk and see if we see anything. If not, you go get the others."

They hurried down the path toward the boardwalk, calling all the way. The boardwalk was empty and woods quiet. Frannie stopped.

"Sally, can you make a cowbird call?"

"Of course! I learned bird calls in Girl Scouts." She began a distinct whistle and continued it as they walked along the boardwalk, looking in every direction.

Frannie kept silent, listening. They had just about reached the cave when she heard it—an answering call. Maybe it was an actual cowbird, but maybe not. She stopped and looked at Sally.

Sally whistled again. The same response, coming from below them. And then a very faint voice. "Sally?"

"She's below us," Frannie whispered. "You go. But be careful—it's awfully steep."

Sally climbed over the railing on the cliff side, carefully searching for footholds. The ground sloped fairly sharply under the walk. She disappeared.

Frannie could hear her moving back the way they had come. "Lyssa?" she said softly. "It's me—Sally."

The little girl began to cry.

Sally called up. "Mom? I've got her. She's all scraped up. I'm going to hand her up to you."

Frannie leaned over the railing and Sally appeared with Lyssa in her arms. The slope was rather rocky and she was having trouble keeping her footing. "Lyssa, this is my mom. I'm going to hand you up to her so I can climb up, okay?"

Lyssa cried more. She shook her head and hugged Sally's neck tighter. "Just for a minute and then I will hold you again. Please? Your momma is very worried about you."

Rocks tumbled down the slope under Sally's feet. She gently removed Lyssa's arms, one at a time from the grip on her neck. "You just count to ten and then make a cowbird whistle and by that time I will be beside you, okay?"

Lyssa slowly started to count. Sally lifted her under her arms up toward Frannie's waiting hands. Just as

Frannie grasped the child, Sally started to slip. She disappeared beneath the boardwalk.

Frannie caught her breath as she clutched the little girl. "Sal? Are you okay?"

A moment's pause and Sally said faintly, "Be right there."

Together Frannie and Lyssa reached out their hands to help Sally up. All three collapsed on a bench built into the rail of the walk. Sally started to laugh and Lyssa joined her, climbing back into Sally's lap.

Frannie smiled and shook her head in amazement at her daughter's mature reaction to the whole situation. The same girl who had been teasing her brother, sticking out her tongue, and whining about doing dishes a couple of hours before. Wonders would never cease.

They made their way back to the campground as expeditiously as possible, which wasn't too fast since Sally had to carry Lyssa and needed to stop frequently. At the river they met Larry.

"Oh good! You found her!" He tried to take Lyssa from Sally. She would have none of it.

"It's okay, Dad. It's not much farther," Sally said between breaths.

He shrugged and dropped back to walk with Frannie. " A young guy named Tim—camped in that pickup?— just came out and said he had seen her head down this trail. He thought she was catching up with her parents or something. He's a botanist and had been out photographing specimens or something."

"Oh," Frannie said, inwardly embarrassed by her speculations. "Well, our daughter saved the day. I'm terribly proud of her."

"Are you guys talkin' about me?" Sally said over her shoulder. Lyssa giggled.

"Only good things," Larry said.

They emerged from the trees to find the ranger and Lyssa's parents talking with a man in sheriff's garb.

Scruffy Guy, Sam and Mona, and Jane Ann stood on the fringes.

Sam spotted them first. "They've got her!"

Lyssa's parents ran up to them and Sally thankfully relinquished the little girl to her mother. Sally then leaned against her own mother and looked up at her with tears in her eyes. Frannie squeezed her and said, "Time to celebrate."

AND A CELEBRATION IT WAS. Sally and Lyssa sat side by side on the picnic bench. Lyssa leaned on Sally and watched the people around her with wide eyes and no other expression. Lyssa's dad, Dennis, went in to town for hot dogs and buns.

Mickey took over as cook. The ranger, Scruffy Guy — Tim—, the Ferraros, and the Shoemakers all gathered around Dennis and Teri's picnic table for dogs, chips, and beans, followed by Frannie's brownies. By the end of supper, Lyssa's eyes were drooping and everyone took their leave.

Back at their own fire, Jane Ann said to Sally, "We

were so proud of you today. That was wonderful how you found Lyssa."

"Mom was the one who thought about using a bird call."

Jane Ann patted Frannie on the knee. "Nice goin', sister-in-law."

"Did Lyssa tell you why she took off like that?" Frannie asked.

Sally shook her head. "The only thing she would tell me was that she climbed on the railing of the boardwalk and slipped off. Good thing she wasn't hurt worse. I think maybe she heard a bird and tried to follow it, but her sight isn't good enough."

"Well, it's been quite a day," Mickey said. "I'm ready for s'mores." He raised his eyebrows at his daughters.

"Your turn to get the stuff out," Mona said to Justine.

"I did it last night."

Mickey cleared his throat. "Girls! Maybe you could make it a team effort so it wouldn't be *so* difficult?"

They caught his drift, giggled, and got out of their chairs.

Mickey strummed some background tunes on his guitar and the kids enjoyed their s'mores like six-year-olds.

Frannie felt totally relaxed and was ready to call it a night, when Sally said in a loud whisper, "What is that?"

Justine looked where she was pointing. "A cat?"

Sam started to laugh. "Try calling it, Jus'. 'Here kitty, kitty.'"

Justine looked at him puzzled. "What?"

"It's a skunk," Sam said.

The adults all sat up and stared into the dark. "Where?"

"It just ran under our trailer."

Larry jumped up. "What? Sam, we don't want a skunk under there! Anything that alarms him is going to stink up the whole camper!"

An older man came walking along the campground road just then, with a small, shaggy dog. The dog stiffened as they approached and began to growl. It strained on its leash toward the Shoemaker trailer.

"Uh-oh," Mickey said, and put down his guitar.

The man tried to coax the dog on down the road, but she was having none of it. Mickey explained what was attracting her interest. The man paled and scooped up the little dog. He hurried down the road with the squirming bundle in his arms.

"Now what?" Larry said to Mickey. "I don't think any of us should go in there, do you?"

Mickey shook his head. "Let's wait a bit. Maybe he'll come back out."

"Sam," Larry said, "move your lawn chair back there where you can see the rear of the trailer."

"Okay, but Sally has to bring me s'mores."

"I'm not going back there!"

Larry showed Sam where to place his chair so that they could still see him and he could see the back of the camper. Sally agreed to go that far to deliver s'mores. She picked up a stick from the woodpile just in case.

Mickey took up his guitar again. "I've been working on a couple of cowboy songs. This is an old Roy Rogers song called 'The Cowboy Night Herd Song.'"

Larry sat back down in his chair and groaned. "C'mon, Mick. We've got enough stress without cowboy songs."

But Mickey was not easily daunted. He sang a couple of verses, and then said, "This is the hard part."

"Oh, Lord, he's going to yodel," Jane Ann said.

Sure enough, he began to yodel the chorus as a pickup truck came around the corner and stopped, pinning the group in its headlights. A park ranger got out, just as Sam jumped up and yelled "There he goes!"

Mickey put the guitar down while Larry doubled over in laughter. "That skunk obviously doesn't care for your yodeling, Mick!"

The ranger reached them. "Sounds like you folks are enjoying your evening,"

Mona overcame her usual shyness around strangers. "Dad just scared a skunk away with his singing!"

"A skunk?"

"One ran under our camper," Frannie said, pointing. "We didn't know how to get it out of there without it spraying. It just ran out when Mickey was singing." She too could not keep from laughing.

The ranger looked at the camper and smiled. "It was

probably my headlights. They don't like bright lights."

"No, we're sure it was Dad's singing," Justine insisted, and giggled.

Mickey threw up his hands. "Greatness is never appreciated."

"Well, have a nice night," the ranger said, and chuckled as he returned to his truck.

Frannie got up and folded her chair. "Okay, I'm not sleepy any more, but I'm going to bed anyway before anything else happens."

The kids wanted to stay around the fire, but Frannie insisted they help her set up their beds first. That chore was not without its hitches. The couch opened up easily enough, but lowering and securing the dinette table was a little trickier. Finally, Sam and Sally were able to spread out their sleeping bags and pillows and return outside.

Frannie and Larry got into bed. Just as she was about to drift off, Larry said, "Don't leave me."

"What?"

"It's been a tough couple of days. But promise you won't leave me if I say I want to keep camping?"

She snorted, trying to hold in the giggles, but couldn't control it. The bed started to shake, and Frannie let loose with a coyote-like howl.

"Hush!" Larry said, and laughed even louder. They heard the outside door open.

"Mom? Are you okay?" Sally asked.

"Fine. We're just discussing our next camping trip." And they both broke up again.

"You're disgusting. I think you two had too much wine," Sally said.

"Yes, Mom," they both said.

Sally waved them off and went back outside.

"Seriously," Larry propped his head up on his hand. "The problems yesterday were all our own fault—we'll learn. And what happened today with the runaway child —that'll probably never happen again. But it *is* a great getaway, especially with our jobs."

"I know—it's easier to deal with our own two kids than one hundred other people's eighth graders."

"And I don't have to worry about any crime sprees or lawbreakers."

"So true." Frannie snuggled into his arm.

THANK YOU, READERS!

Larry may have been too hasty in dismissing crimes and lawbreakers. Follow the adventures of the Shoemakers and their friends in the Frannie Shoemaker Campground Mysteries. All of the books include recipes and camping tips. Reviews on Amazon and Goodreads are much appreciated.

Get the first one, *Bats and Bones*, FREE if you sign up for my Favorite Readers email list to receive occasional notices about my new books and special offers.

Go to this link:
        www.karenmussernortman.com

HAPPY CAMPER TIPS

The Frannie Shoemaker Mysteries include camping hints and recipes--great for camping but also at home. Here's a sample:

Happy Camper Tip #1

Jane Ann's Cowboy Beans: Brown 1lb. hamburger with a diced medium onion. After browning, add 1 can each of drained black beans, pinto beans, white beans, and pork and beans. Then add 1/2 cup ketchup, 1/3 cup brown sugar, 1/4 cup yellow mustard, 3T of Worcestershire sauce and a few dashes of hot sauce. Place in Dutch oven and over campfire for about an hour or two till nice and hot, or in crock pot for 4 hours on low.-- Julie Biver

Happy Camper Tip #2

Shut It! Frannie and Larry ran into trouble because one of the faucets wasn't turned off. This happened to us on our second trip. And Frannie didn't latch the refrigerator tightly causing a huge mess. Many campers have had the gross experience of starting to dump their tanks and taking the cap off the sewer hose housing to find the individual dump valves aren't closed. Not good. Open windows or vents while traveling can cause other problems. And if you wonder what can happen if you travel without shutting and locking your outside compartments, read The Space Invader. So, as I said, Shut it!

Acknowledgments

To all of my readers who sent accounts of their camping experiences and my Beta readers: Butch, Marcia, Ginge, Elaine, Julie, and Dee who made great suggestions and catches. Also to our own camping buddies for providing some of the inspiration.

About the Author

Karen Musser Nortman is the author of the Frannie Shoemaker Campground cozy mystery series, including the BRAGMedallion honoree, *Bats and Bones*. After previous incarnations as a secondary social studies teacher (22 years) and a test developer (18 years), she returned to her childhood dream of writing a novel. The Frannie Shoemaker Campground Mysteries came out of numerous 'round the campfire' discussions, making up answers to questions raised by the peephole glimpses one gets into the lives of fellow campers. Where did those people disappear to for the last two days? What kinds of bones are in this fire pit? Why is that woman wearing heels to the shower house?

Karen and her husband Butch originally tent camped when their children were young and switched to a travel trailer when sleeping on the ground lost its romantic adventure. They take frequent weekend jaunts with friends to parks in Iowa and surrounding states, plus occasional longer trips. Entertainment on these trips has ranged from geocaching and hiking/biking to barbecue contests, balloon fests, and buck skinners' rendezvous.

Sign up for Karen's email list at www.karenmussernortman.com and receive a free ereader download of *Bats and Bones*.

Other Books by the Author

THE AWARD-WINNING FRANNIE SHOEMAKER CAMPGROUND MYSTERIES:

The Frannie Shoemaker Campground Mystery Series: INDIE BRAG MEDALLION HONOREES. *Camping can be murder. Oh, sure, there's the stunning scenery, socializing with old friends and new acquaintances, amazing food cooked outside, and so on. But what if a dead body turns up on one of your hikes-for-fun-and fitness?* For more information and other books, check my website: www.karenmussernortman.com

Bats and Bones: A Fourth of July weekend explodes with more than fireworks when the campground hostess is found dead.

The Blue Coyote: Frannie worries more than usual about her grandchildren's safety when another young girl disappears from the campground in broad daylight.

Peete and Repeat: A biking and camping trip to southeastern Minnesota turns into double trouble for Frannie Shoemaker and her friends.

The Lady of the Lake: Frannie Shoemaker and her friends take in the county fair, reminisce at a Fifties-Sixties dance, and check out old hangouts. A trip down memory lane is fine if you don't stumble on a body.

To Cache a Killer: Geocaching isn't supposed to be about finding dead bodies. But when retiree Frannie Shoemaker goes camping, standard definitions don't apply.

A Campy Christmas: No murder but definitely a mystery when the Shoemakers and Ferraros become snowbound in a Missouri park on their way to spend Christmas in Texas.

The Space Invader: A cozy/thriller mystery! The starry skies over New Mexico, the "Land of Enchantment," may hold secrets of their own. The Shoemakers and the Ferraros, on an extended camping trip, find themselves picking up a souvenir they don't want and taking sidetrips they didn't plan on.

Happy Camper Tips and Recipes: All of the tips and recipes from the first four Frannie Shoemaker books in one convenient paperback or Kindle version that you can keep in your camping supplies.

THE TIME TRAVEL TRAILER SERIES

The Time Travel Trailer: (An IndieBRAG Medallion honoree, 2015 Chanticleer Paranormal First-in-Category winner) Lynne McBriar decides to try camping to reconnect with her teenage daughter and finds a 1937 vintage camper trailer half hidden in weeds. But camping in the trailer takes them on adventures they never imagined.

Trailer on the Fly: Lynne McBriar meets a young woman who suffers from serious depression over the loss of a close friend ten years earlier, and must decide whether to use the Time Travel Trailer to back and change events.

Trailer, Get Your Kicks! Lynne and her family take the Time Travel Trailer on Route 66 in 1952. Several unexpected twists make the journey more dangerous than they bargained for.